A SWORD FOR JOAN OF ARC

Sam Godwin

Illustrated by
Kay Dixey

Joan of Arc – Timeline

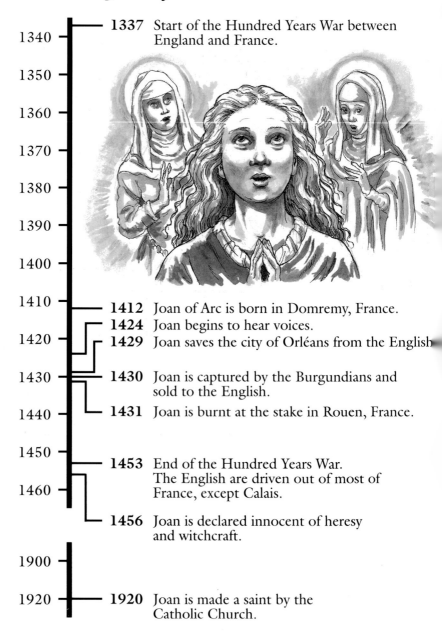

1340	**1337**	Start of the Hundred Years War between England and France.
1350		
1360		
1370		
1380		
1390		
1400		
1410	**1412**	Joan of Arc is born in Domremy, France.
1420	**1424**	Joan begins to hear voices.
	1429	Joan saves the city of Orléans from the English
1430	**1430**	Joan is captured by the Burgundians and sold to the English.
1440	**1431**	Joan is burnt at the stake in Rouen, France.
1450	**1453**	End of the Hundred Years War. The English are driven out of most of France, except Calais.
1460		
	1456	Joan is declared innocent of heresy and witchcraft.
1900		
1920	**1920**	Joan is made a saint by the Catholic Church.

Chapter 1

I smiled at the girl who'd just come into
our bakery. 'What can I do for you, Marie?'

'I'll have two loaves of bread,' said the
girl, 'and a biscuit, please.' Marie reminded
me of myself when I was young. Like her,
I was mad about biscuits then. Luckily, my
mother made the best biscuits in Domremy.

'Papa's just come back from Paris,'
said Marie as I put the fresh loaves in her
basket. 'He heard that the court has found
Joan of Arc innocent of all her crimes.'

Even after all these years, the very mention of Joan's name filled me with a mixture of pride and pain – but mostly pain. 'It will do her no good now,' I said sadly. 'She's been dead for twenty-five years.'

'Papa said they're going to build a monument for her in town,' continued Marie. 'He says they're probably going to have statues of Joan all over France.'

I frowned. 'No amount of monuments will bring Joan back.'

'My teacher says Joan's story is the stuff of legend,' Marie chattered on. 'A country girl, just like me, leads the French army against the invading English. She wins one battle after another. Until one day she is caught, found guilty of witchcraft and burnt at the stake.'

'Joan was no witch,' I said, handing the loaves to Marie. 'She was a saint.'

'Papa told me she must have been very ambitious to get to see the King,' went on Marie. 'A girl has to be really ambitious to lead an army.'

'Joan? Ambitious?' I couldn't help laughing. 'Never. Marie, all Joan ever wanted was a quiet life in the country. It was mysterious voices that told her to fight the English. In the end she had no choice but to try and see the King. And we all know where that led.'

'You seem to know a lot about Joan of Arc,' said Marie. 'Did you know her?'

I put my hands on my hips and beamed at the little girl. 'Mademoiselle,' I said proudly. 'My name is Hauviette. I was Joan of Arc's best friend. I can tell you everything about her…'

Chapter 2

It was a hot summer afternoon. Joan and I and another friend called Mengette were sitting on the grass near the Fairy Tree. That's an old beech tree on the outskirts of the village. People say it's the home of spirits and, if you believe in them, fairies. Mengette held up a garland of flowers. 'Shall I hang it on the branches?' she asked.

'Why not?' I said, sitting back on the warm, summer grass, 'we always hang our garlands on the Fairy Tree.'

'Joan says it's not right,' said Mengette. 'Isn't that true, Joan?'

Joan, who was lying on the grass beside me, sat up. 'That's what the priest told me,' she said. 'We shouldn't look to the forest spirits for help. We should pray to God and the saints.'

'But people have been coming to the Fairy Tree for hundreds of years,' argued Mengette. 'They come to draw water from the fountain too. My mum says it's got healing powers.'

'That might be true,' said Joan, 'but the priest says…'

Just then we heard something trundling down the country road. 'What's that?' I asked, standing up to have a better look.

'Refugees from the north,' said Joan, 'They must have been turned out of their homes by the English.'

'It's not fair,' I said, watching a thin boy and a girl pushing a cart along the dusty road. 'The English have taken over most of northern France. It'll be our turn soon.'

'There's nothing we can do about it,' sighed Joan. 'The English are too powerful. Our Prince Charles is too weak to fight back.'

'Don't worry,' said Mengette. 'My granny told me there's an old, local prophecy about the English. It says that a girl from around here will drive them out of France.'

'What a silly prophecy,' laughed Joan. 'How can a powerless girl save a whole country?'

Chapter 3

The refugees disappeared round a bend in the road. Mengette hung her garland on the Fairy Tree. 'I should be getting home,' she said. 'I promised Mum I'd help with the darning.'

'Me too,' said Joan. 'I'm making pies for Jacques and Pierre tonight.'

Jacques and Pierre were Joan's elder brothers. They worked with their father out in the fields while Joan stayed at home to help her mother.

'I'll see you two tomorrow,' said Mengette. She hurried along the path, a bunch of firewood held under one arm. Joan and I walked home slowly. Late afternoon was our favourite part of the day. The countryside was quiet. The world seemed to be at peace with itself, and there was the nice cosy evening next to the fire to look forward to. Evenings are chilly in this part of the world, even in summer.

Joan and I said goodnight outside her house. She lived right next to the church, in the only cottage around here with glass in its window.

'I must get some roses from the garden,' Joan said, 'and some herbs for the pies.'

'I'll see you tomorrow, then,' I said, 'at about half past four, after I've done my chores.'

'See you,' said Joan. She waved and disappeared into the garden. I continued down the road, thinking about supper and the new dress my mum was making for me. Then I remembered something. I couldn't see Joan the next day. Mum and I were going to the market to buy buttons. I turned back to tell Joan. She hated it when people didn't stick to their arrangements.

'Joan?' I called out as
I approached her garden.

There was no answer.

'Joan?' I called again.
I could see her kneeling on the grass, a
bunch of roses in her hands. She was
staring at the church across the garden.

'Are you all right?' I shouted. But it was
obvious she hadn't heard me. Suddenly she
dropped the roses. Her hands flew up to
shield her eyes, as if a bright light was
shining in her face.

'I cannot, Monsieur,' she cried. 'I tell
you I cannot.'

'Joan,' I wanted to say, 'who are you talking to? There is no one there.' But somehow the words wouldn't come out of my mouth. I just stood there, unable even to move.

Joan reached out to the skies. 'Take me to Heaven with you,' she sobbed at something or someone only she could see. 'I want to come with you. Don't leave me behind.'

And then she collapsed on the ground.

Chapter 4

'Joan, how long has this been going on?' I asked.

It was two days after the incident in the garden. Joan and I were tucked up in bed. I often spent the night at her house, telling stories well into the early hours of the morning.

'A few years, I think' Joan said. 'I can't really remember when they started.'

'They' were voices that whispered in Joan's head. They belonged to Saint Catherine and Saint Margaret. They told Joan that she had been chosen to save France from the English. First she had to lead the French army to the city of Orléans. Orléans was still in the hands of the French, but only just. According to the voices, Joan was to lead new French troops there to help fight off the English. She was to win the battle at Orléans for them.

'You don't think I'm mad, do you?' continued Joan.

I lay my head gently on her shoulder. I know I should have been puzzled and frightened. After all, here was my best friend, claiming she could win a battle so many famous captains had lost. But I wasn't scared; I was strangely calm, for I felt that Joan really could save France. 'Don't be silly,' I said, 'you're the most sensible person I know.'

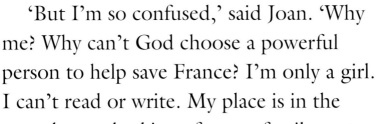

'But I'm so confused,' said Joan. 'Why me? Why can't God choose a powerful person to help save France? I'm only a girl. I can't read or write. My place is in the home, looking after my family, not charging across a battlefield.' She shuddered, clasping her hands around her shoulders. 'I don't even have a sword to fight with.'

'Don't worry, Joan,' I said, 'if God wants you to fight for France, I will pray for him to find you a sword.'

Chapter 5

The way I saw it, Joan had three problems to solve before she could lead an army against the English.

First she had to convince her father that God really did want her to fight the English. Then she had to convince Captain Baudricourt. He was the governor of Vaucouleurs, the nearest town to Domremy. If anyone around here wanted to get in touch with Prince Charles, they had to go to him first.

Finally, of course, she had to convince Prince Charles himself – the Dauphin as he was known – to give her an army. I always thought that would be the tricky one, but in the end it was her father who put up the most resistance. When Joan told him about the voices he nearly had a fit.

'I'll drown you with my own hands
before I let you join the army,' bellowed
her father. He didn't really mean it, of
course. It was his fear talking. Joan was his
only daughter and he wanted the best for her.

Joan's mum locked her up in her room. She wouldn't let her come out, not even to help scrub the floor or cook pies. 'You should be thinking about marriage,' she said, 'not battlefields and danger.'

Joan's father turned to me. 'You run along home, Hauviette,' he said. 'Come back tomorrow. Joan will be fine by then. A night without supper will make her see sense.'

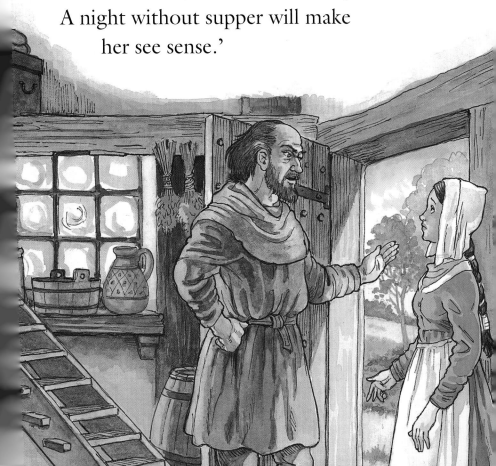

I went home and told my mum what had happened. That was a big mistake. My mum told my aunt and her husband. Soon all of Domremy knew about Joan and her voices. Many people believed her too.

'It's the prophecy,' they said. 'Joan is the one who will save us from the English.'

The next morning I hurried back to
Joan's house. Her parents had let her out
of her room. I think the voices must have
told her something special the night
before. She came down the stairs looking
all calm and confident. Gone was the timid
girl I had known for so many years. In her
place was a brave, young woman.

'Mum and Dad will never help me in my
mission,' she told me, 'but the voices say I
must talk to my uncle. He will make sure
that I am seen by Captain Baudricourt.'

Chapter 6

That was the last time I ever spoke to Joan. A few days later she went to stay with her uncle, who lived not far from here. She stayed with him for some time, mainly to look after her sick aunt who needed some help around the house – or so he told Joan's father. I don't know what Joan said to her uncle, or whether the voices had worked their wonders on him too, but he agreed to take her to Vaucouleurs.

Joan's parents begged her once more
to stay at home. It was no use. Joan had
made up her mind. She kissed Mengette
good-bye. Mengette told her to come and
see me too but Joan didn't have the heart.
She knew that we would
miss each other too much.
So she travelled to
Vaucouleurs without
ever saying good-bye
to me, in a red dress
made by her mother.

31

I heard the rest of the story from Joan's uncle. He said that, at first, Captain Baudricourt refused to see Joan again. But they persisted and, after a while, they succeeded in seeing the Captain.

Joan told him all about her voices. 'You must send me to see the Dauphin,' she said, 'for I am destined to save France.'

The Captain laughed out loud. 'How can a girl, and a peasant girl at that, save a noble country from heartless invaders?' he said. 'Go back home to your cooking and cleaning, little girl. Leave the fighting to the men.'

But the Captain's advisers had heard all about Joan. She was becoming famous all over the region. 'Give her a chance,' they begged the Captain, 'she might be our country's last hope.'

Baudricourt was adamant. 'No,' he said.

Chapter 7

Joan was disappointed by the Captain's decision. But she returned to his castle in winter. Her uncle told me that the voices had spoken to her again. 'Be patient,' they said, 'you will see the King before Easter.'

This time, Captain Baudricourt sent Joan to see his friend the Duke of Lorraine. The Duke was sick and was hoping that Joan, with her closeness to God, could heal him. Joan stayed with him for a while. She talked to him about the voices and what they had said was in store for her.

'Will the Captain not
send word to the
Dauphin?' asked the Duke.
'It seems such a shame to
turn down God's help.'

'Never fear,' said Joan,
'I shall see the Dauphin.
And I shall win Orléans
for us.'

But the Duke was not as optimistic as Joan was. He knew that it was almost impossible to gain an audience with the Dauphin. Many people and even famous dukes like him had been turned away from court. What chance had a simple peasant girl?

But the Duke hadn't taken into account the power of the voices in Joan's head. Meanwhile, fearing the worsening situation in Orléans, Captain Baudricourt had secretly written to the Dauphin. 'Would his majesty see a girl who claims she can win France back from the English?'

The Dauphin's first reaction was to say no. He didn't like ordinary people and believed that there were enough fools in court without adding a holy peasant girl to them. Then he had some bad news. Another battle against the English had been lost. The enemy had taken more territory from him and killed more Frenchmen.

'Perhaps I should
see this girl,' he told
his advisors. 'It seems
to me there is nothing
to lose.'

So Joan was called back to Vaucouleurs
immediately. Her supporters had managed
to raise some money. They bought her
a horse and saddle, and a soldier's suit
of armour.

I happened to be in town that day. I saw Joan emerging from the Captain's castle, ready to set off for the Dauphin's court in Chinon. She had six men with her, also dressed in armour.

Joan didn't see me. I was lost in the crowds. But I saw her very clearly. She didn't look scared. No, she looked brave, just like a soldier.

I clapped and cheered as she passed by. Captain Baudricourt had made my own little prayer come true, you see. He'd given Joan a parting gift. A sword.

Joan of Arc was born in Domremy, a small village in France in 1412. The Hundred Years War between England and France had been raging for seventy-five years and the English occupied most of France. Joan, called Jeanette by her friends and family was 12 or 13 when she started hearing voices and having visions. She claimed that St Catherine, St Margaret and later St Michael, kept telling her to go to the help of the Dauphin, the uncrowned King of France. They told her that she would drive the English out of France and see the Dauphin crowned.

Eventually, the Dauphin let her lead an army to the city of Orléans, which the English had been attacking for five months. Joan succeeded in driving the English away from Orléans. Then she led her troops to more and more victories. When the Dauphin was crowned King Charles VII in 1429, Joan was considered a National hero. The next year Joan was captured by the Burgundians (French traitors who sided with the English). They sold her to the English. Joan was put on trial as a traitor and a witch and burnt at the stake in 1431. In 1456, a new court in Paris found Joan innocent of all her crimes and in 1920 she was declared a saint by the Roman Catholic Church. May 8 is still a national holiday in France because it is the day, in 1429, that Joan of Arc captured Orléans.